OFF ROAD

RAELYN DRAKE

darbycreek
MINNEAPOLIS

Darby Creek
A division of Lerner Publishing Group, Inc.
241 First Avenue North
Minneapolis, MN 55401 USA

For reading levels and more information, look up this title at
www.lernerbooks.com.

Cover and interior images: LongQuattro/Shutterstock.com (tire track grunge); Alan Poulson Photography/Shutterstock.com (biker); grop/Shutterstock.com (forest outline).

Main body text set in Janson Text LT Std.
Typeface provided by Adobe Systems.

Library of Congress Cataloging-in-Publication Data

Names: Drake, Raelyn, author.
Title: Off road / Raelyn Drake.
Description: Minneapolis : Darby Creek, [2019] | Series: To the limit | Summary:
    Best friends Tanika and Wyatt face great danger when disaster strikes during a
    day-long mountain biking trip on unfamiliar trails.
Identifiers: LCCN 2018019484 (print) | LCCN 2018036303 (ebook) |
    ISBN 9781541541986 (eb pdf) | ISBN 9781541540354 (lb : alk. paper) |
    ISBN 9781541545533 (pb : alk. paper)
Subjects: | CYAC: Mountain biking—Fiction. | Bicycles and bicycling—Fiction. |
    Best friends—Fiction. | Friendship—Fiction. | Survival—Fiction. | Forests and
    forestry—Fiction.
Classification: LCC PZ7.1.D74 (ebook) | LCC PZ7.1.D74 Off 2019 (print) | DDC
    [Fic]—dc23

LC record available at https://lccn.loc.gov/2018019484

Manufactured in the United States of America
1-45240-36622-8/16/2018

For my parents, who inspired my love of
the Pacific Northwest

CHAPTER ONE

Wyatt pumped the pedals of his mountain bike, his lungs burning as he neared the scenic overlook at the peak of the mountain.

He and his friend Tanika had almost finished the grueling ride up the side of the mountain, zigzagging back and forth along the paved hiking path in the scorching midday sun to get to where the actual mountain bike trail started.

With one last burst of energy, Wyatt reached the top of the trail and coasted to a stop at the stone wall that ran around the edge of the overlook. He flipped out the kickstand on his bike and took off his helmet. The cool mountain breeze was a welcome relief. Wyatt's hair was matted with sweat.

Tanika grinned as she parked her bike next to Wyatt's. "Would you look at that view!" she exclaimed.

"We should come here again," Wyatt said.

This was their first time at Evergreen Wilds Park. Their usual park was way too crowded now that it was summer vacation, and they'd heard that Evergreen Wilds had some great trails. And more importantly, it had fewer tourists. The view of the forested mountainside was definitely worth it so far, Wyatt had to admit. He grabbed a couple of granola bars and oranges out of his backpack, and they sat on the stone wall to eat.

"Let's not get too comfortable," Tanika said after a while. She stood up, cramming the last of her orange in her mouth. "Like you said earlier, we should try to make it back before dark."

Wyatt looked at the dense forest around them. It was beautiful, but in the span of just their short break, the beating sun had been replaced with overcast skies. Even though it was still early afternoon, the sky was getting darker as fog was starting to cover the pine trees about halfway down the mountain. There had been heavy rain the day before, and Wyatt hoped that today's rain would hold off until they got home—or at least off the trails.

Rain or no rain, Wyatt was just as eager to get going as Tanika. Riding uphill had been slow and sweaty. But the downhill ride, with its exhilarating speed and jumps, would make it well worth it.

There were three mountain bike trails that led down the mountain—one easier beginner trail marked with green signs, an intermediate-level path that was a little bit more challenging indicated with blue, and the advanced yellow path a little ways farther.

"So do you want to go on the green or blue trail?" Wyatt asked as he put on his helmet and tightened the chinstrap.

Tanika scoffed. "Beginner or intermediate? I was hoping for a real challenge. Why not the black diamond?"

Wyatt looked over at the yellow trail marker indicating the advanced black diamond path and then back over at Tanika cautiously. "Seriously?" She was usually more confident than he was when it came to their ability, but this seemed extreme, even for her.

"Yeah, why not?" Tanika responded defensively. She took out her water bottle and took a few swigs.

"You should save more of your water," Wyatt said, stalling.

Tanika rolled her eyes. "I still have a third of the bottle left. It's not going to take us *that* long to bike back to the car." She took another swig and then stashed it in the water bottle holder on her bike. Wyatt took a small sip of his water and carefully returned the bottle to his backpack.

Then he pulled out his phone to look at the trail map he had a screenshot of from the park website. "Look, I'm still a little tired from the ride up. Can we check out the intermediate trail first?" he asked, pointing at the blue line weaving down the mountainside on the map.

"We'll cross the black diamond trail a little ways down the mountain. If we do well on the intermediate trail up until that point, maybe we can branch off to take the advanced path the rest of the way down."

Tanika sighed but nodded her agreement. She looked over his shoulder at the map. "What's that gray section?"

Wyatt tapped the screen to zoom in. "It says 'out of bounds.' I guess they want us to stay on the marked trails."

Tanika smirked. "Yeah, like I'm going to miss all the cool obstacles on the trails so I can go ride through poison ivy and mountain lion scat in the woods." She patted her jacket pocket and grimaced.

"What's wrong?" Wyatt asked.

Tanika sighed. "I just realized I forgot my phone . . . again."

Wyatt tried not to roll his eyes. Tanika always seemed to be forgetting her phone somewhere, especially when they were getting ready to go mountain biking. "Where'd you leave it?"

"I think it must be back in the car," Tanika muttered. "Because I was texting on the drive here, but now I don't have it. I must have forgotten to go back and grab it after we got our bikes off the back of your car." She kicked a pebble on the ground, frowning.

"Hey, no big deal, these things happen," Wyatt said, trying to keep the annoyance out of his voice. "We have my phone in case of emergencies."

Tanika gave him a small smile. "This is why I keep you around, Wy."

Her grateful look made Wyatt feel guilty for getting annoyed with his friend. *It really isn't that big of a deal*, he reminded himself. They probably wouldn't need a phone anyway, and if they did, they had his.

Tanika hopped on her bike and gestured to the blue trail marker. "You first," she said. She was grinning now, the embarrassment of forgetting her phone replaced by eager anticipation of the ride ahead.

Wyatt returned her grin and started down the trail, pedaling hard to gain some initial momentum. Then as the trail sloped downward and gravity took over, Wyatt shifted forward and coasted.

The trail twisted and curved down the side of the mountain, cutting a narrow path through the woods. It would rise and fall in a series of gentle waves, then curve sharply so that Wyatt had to lean into the bend so much that his handlebars were inches away from the dirt. It was like being on a roller coaster.

Wyatt savored the adrenaline rush. The trail was really living up to the hype. If this was the intermediate trail, Wyatt was tempted to try the advanced trail. Tanika would definitely want to give it a run, but even Wyatt was pretty sure they could handle it.

They had been riding bikes together since sixth grade, and while Tanika was a fearless rider, Wyatt always had the nagging thought in the back of his mind that something could go wrong at any moment. His caution prevented him from wiping out as much as Tanika did, but sometimes he wished he could just shut off his anxiety and truly enjoy the moment as he was riding. Whenever the trail dipped without warning, it was hard to tell if the fluttering in his stomach was fear or excitement.

A flash of orange caught his eye to the left—a sign on the side of the trail to indicate the first big jump takeoff.

Wyatt's heart beat a little faster as he pedaled to accelerate, visualizing himself landing the jump perfectly. He leaned forward into the ramp, then shifted his weight from his hands to his feet, his body uncoiling like a spring as his bike left the ground. He felt the weightlessness of flight and then the landing of a perfect jump.

Wyatt grinned, feeling more confident about the bike ride now that he had warmed up on that first jump. He continued down the trail, hearing Tanika whoop excitedly as she hit the jump behind him.

They sped down the mountain, and after his third successful jump, he was starting to feel much more relaxed on the unfamiliar trail and got into the flow. He usually didn't like to ride blind on an unknown trail, but this trail was well marked with signs to indicate the next challenge. And besides, he was enjoying himself too much to worry.

Wyatt rounded a bend in the trail and his heart dropped as he saw that the trail in front of them was a mess of mud and twigs and rocks. He skidded to a stop with a warning shout. Tanika braked hard behind him, nearly losing control of her bike.

"Yesterday's rain must have washed the trail out," Wyatt said. "We have to get off our bikes and walk to make it through."

Tanika groaned. "That will take forever. There's hardly any trail left. The rain swept half of it down the mountainside." She looked around and pointed at a second trail that branched off from the main trail. "That part looks much drier."

Wyatt looked where she was pointing. The second trail was narrower, but it certainly looked safer than the swampy main trail.

"Didn't you say the advanced trail connects with the intermediate trail?" Tanika asked. "I bet this is it."

Wyatt bit his lip in thought. "Maybe . . ." he said.

"If we try to get through that muck on the intermediate trail, it will be dark by the time we actually get back," Tanika pointed out.

Wyatt glanced at the dense trees around them. In the overcast afternoon light, the woods had started to look gloomy.

"Wouldn't it be marked though?" he asked. "They don't want anybody accidentally ending up on the advanced trail if they weren't ready for it. I don't see a sign anywhere."

Tanika huffed. "I'm *sure* it's the black diamond trail. But if you don't believe me, then fine," she said, her voice heavy with sarcasm. "Waste our time by getting the trail map out to double check."

Wyatt prickled at Tanika's mocking tone. *He* wasn't nearly as confident that it was the trail. But he had to admit that it was a clear path branching off the intermediate trail, just like he had seen on the trail map.

Wyatt thought about checking his phone anyway, but Tanika was already staring at him impatiently. She always said that he worried too much. *Maybe she has a point*, he thought.

Besides, he didn't really want to spend an hour slogging through the mud when he could be flying down the mountain on his bike.

"Fine," he said at last. "But don't get overconfident. We have no idea what the jumps and obstacles are like on this course."

"Yeah, yeah, I know the drill," Tanika said. "I'll go first this time, and I'll take it easy. I promise," she said. But the grin on her face made Wyatt seriously doubt it.

The new trail was much steeper and rockier, and whenever he jolted over a rough patch, Wyatt had to fight to keep control of the bike. He was glad he had let Tanika go ahead of him. He knew she was probably going way too fast, but at least he had a heads up whenever he was approaching a big jump or obstacle.

Wyatt thought it was a little strange that the obstacles on this trail weren't marked with colorful signs like before. But Wyatt hadn't been on a lot of advanced trails. Maybe the lack of signs was part of the challenge on a difficult course.

Either way, he wasn't enjoying the ride as much as he normally did. He made an effort to loosen his white-knuckle grip on the handlebars as the trail plunged steeply. He tried to brake lightly, but he was still picking up speed like crazy. At the bottom of the hill, the trail curved so much it nearly doubled back on itself.

He saw Tanika's bike wobble dangerously as she launched herself off a rock that jutted out in the middle of the path. Wyatt made a split-second decision that he wasn't up for a jump like that and steered his bike to the side of the rock.

He hadn't seen the tree root next to the rock. The impact as he hit it jarred him so hard he felt his teeth rattle, and before Wyatt could even register the fact that he was crashing, it was already too late.

CHAPTER TWO

The treetops and the ground swapped places, and Wyatt tried to bail from his bike as he realized he was flying through the air. But his leg caught the edge of the bike and turned his controlled fall into a dizzying somersault. He hit the ground so hard it knocked the breath out of him. His bike stopped tumbling, but the hill was so steep that Wyatt slid and rolled another thirty feet before coming to a stop.

He wasn't sure how long he lay on his back, sucking in shallow, panicky breaths and staring up at the little patches of pale gray sky that were visible between the branches above him.

The trees seemed to be spinning, and Wyatt couldn't decide if that was just normal dizziness or if he had hit his head.

It took a moment for the reality of the crash to set in. When it did, he became aware of something running through the undergrowth toward him. Someone shouted his name, and he realized it was Tanika.

"Are you all right?!" she shouted as she got closer. "Wyatt?" She dropped to her knees next to him. "*Wyatt*? Hey, talk to me. Talk to me so I know you're okay."

Wyatt wasn't sure he had ever heard Tanika sound so worried before. "I'm fine," he said, although it came out as more of a croak.

Tanika's words tumbled out in a rush. "I heard you scream and then there was this awful thud and when I turned around I couldn't even see you because you had gone off the side of the trail, and I found your bike all smashed up—"

Wyatt blinked a couple of times. He hadn't even realized he *had* screamed.

"—but at first I couldn't find you," Tanika continued, "so of course I was freaking out, but I saw your neon blue jacket through the trees, thank goodness. Do you think you can sit up?"

Wyatt groaned at the thought, but unless he was numb from shock, he didn't think he had seriously injured himself. He slowly pushed himself up with Tanika's help. He was going to have some serious bruises and his ribs were a little tender, but he could move his arms and legs without too much pain, and it didn't hurt when he turned his head side to side.

"Your helmet isn't cracked, so hopefully that means you didn't hit your head too hard," Tanika remarked. "How many fingers am I holding up?" she asked, and held up a closed fist with mock seriousness.

Wyatt snorted. "Zero," he said, rolling his eyes.

Tanika's mischievous laugh cut off abruptly and her eyes went wide. "Wyatt, you're bleeding."

Wyatt saw now that at some point in his fall he had cut up his arm. The sleeve of his jacket had been ripped to shreds and beneath it there was a long gash on his arm. It ran from his shoulder to his elbow and oozed dark red blood.

"Ugh," Wyatt groaned.

"We'll need to get that cleaned out," Tanika said. Now that she seemed to be over her initial fear for Wyatt's safety, Wyatt was impressed at how calm and collected she sounded. But his friend had always been good in a crisis. Wyatt just hoped that if he spent enough time preparing, he wouldn't have to deal with a crisis at all.

But this trip wasn't exactly going according to plan.

"I have a small first aid kit in the side pocket of my backpack," Wyatt said. He leaned forward gingerly so that Tanika could access his backpack and winced at the stinging pain in his arm and ribs.

Tanika sorted through the contents of the first aid kit. "It's not much more than a few bandages, some cotton balls, a roll of gauze, a small pair of scissors, and some antibiotic ointment," she said.

"Better than nothing," Wyatt said.

Tanika poured the last of the water in her water bottle over the wound to wash away the dirt and debris. Wyatt gritted his teeth against the pain, but he was relieved to see once the cut was clean that it actually wasn't as bad as he had first thought. It sure hurt a lot, and he would probably have a scar, but at least he wasn't going to bleed out in the middle of the woods. Not yet, anyway.

Tanika had him hold his arm up over his head until the worst of the bleeding stopped and then wrapped his injured arm in gauze.

"You look like a mummy," Tanika said with a snicker. "Or at least your bandaged arm does. Do you think you can stand?" she asked, going from funny Tanika to calm-in-a-crisis Tanika like flipping a switch. "We should try to get back up to the main trail. I'll grab your bike from the bushes on the way and we can see what kind of shape it's in."

Wyatt clipped his helmet to his backpack and then looked up the steep incline he had tumbled down. Just the thought of climbing back up it made him groan, but he knew they couldn't just stay at the bottom of the hill.

Making it back up to the trail was difficult without the full use of one of his arms. He didn't seem to have twisted or broken anything, but the cut stung and sent sharp jabs of pain shooting up his arm if he moved it too suddenly or tried to use it to pull himself up the incline. With Tanika's help, Wyatt managed to scramble back up to the trail, grabbing exposed tree roots and jutting rocks to keep his balance at such a steep angle.

Wyatt could still hardly believe that he had fallen that far after losing his bike. Exhausted and in pain, Wyatt sat down heavily on a rock on the side of the trail and examined the rest of his scrapes and bruises while Tanika lugged his bike back up.

Wyatt had never had any problem reading Tanika's expressions, and now as she returned with his bike he could easily see that she was nervous about something. Which meant only one thing.

"How bad is the damage?" Wyatt called.

"Umm . . . let's just say that it's *not* great," Tanika said, dragging the bike over and propping it up against a nearby tree. She sighed and wrinkled her nose. "Not great at all."

Wyatt felt a stab of pain almost worse than the pain in his arm when he looked at his beloved mountain bike and saw the mangled metal frame. The seat was tilted at an angle, the wheel spokes were bent, and the front tire had been punctured in at least five places.

Tanika took off her helmet, ran a hand over her curly hair, and sighed again. "It looks like it was run over by a truck," she said finally.

"Are you sure I hit a root?" Wyatt asked. "Maybe I ran into a deer." He laughed weakly at his own joke, trying to keep the edge of panic out of his voice as he realized just how badly his bike was damaged.

"I'm never going to be able to ride the rest of the way on that," Wyatt said. One look at

Tanika told him that she was thinking the same thing.

Tanika grimaced. "I don't suppose you have a bike repair kit in that backpack of yours?"

"I have a great bike repair kit in the back of the car. Whole lot of good that does me right now," Wyatt said. "All I brought in my backpack is a single tire patch and a pump, but that's not going to be nearly enough."

"So your full kit is miles away that way," Tanika said. She pointed over her shoulder to indicate the general direction of the parking lot, then frowned. "Err, actually I guess the parking lot is . . ." she looked at the trees around them and then swept her hand around in frustration, "somewhere."

"Let's stop kidding ourselves," Wyatt said glumly. "We're not on the right trail. If this were the black diamond trail, that jump should have been clearly marked. And I haven't seen one sign since—" Wyatt paused. He had just seen something orange lying near the side of the trail, half obscured by dead pine needles and moss. "What's that?"

Tanika cleared away the debris and held up the orange warning sign so they could both read it:

BIKE PARK BOUNDARY. NOT PATROLLED. The area beyond this boundary is hazardous backcountry terrain—trails are unmarked and unmaintained. Persons proceeding beyond this point should be equipped and trained for self-rescue and be prepared for dangerous terrain, weather changes, and wildlife encounters.

"If this isn't even an official bike trail, then what is it?" Tanika asked.

"It could be some sort of animal path, I guess," Wyatt said. "I'll get the trail map out."

He reached into the main section of his backpack and froze. It was wet. That wasn't right. Why on Earth was it wet? Wyatt unzipped it all the way to examine the contents. He pulled out his water bottle and discovered that it was dripping. He found a long hole slashed in the side and tried to plug it with his thumb. But the damage was done. The water bottle had already leaked more than half of his water.

"It must have gotten punctured when I crashed and has been slowly leaking since," Wyatt moaned. "Here, hold this," he said, and Tanika took the wet, leaking water bottle from him.

Meanwhile, Wyatt tried to rescue the soaking wet contents of his backpack. He found his phone lying in a puddle of water at the very bottom.

Muttering under his breath, he dried it off with his jacket. It had powered off. "Should I turn it on?" he asked Tanika.

Tanika shook her head. "I wouldn't risk it, unless you want to fry your phone. I'm pretty sure the only way you're going to salvage that thing is if you get it home and leave it in a bag of rice for a couple of days."

"Then how are we supposed to look at the map?" Wyatt said. "You left your phone in the car. Like you always do," he added before he could stop himself.

Tanika scowled. "Yeah, yeah, I know. You don't need to remind me that I screwed up by forgetting it. It's not like I forgot it on purpose. *Obviously* I wish I had my phone with me right now."

"Sorry," Wyatt said. "I'm just trying to think through our options here."

"What options?" Tanika said, still sounding a little annoyed. "Why don't we just head back the way we came until we connect with the main trail?"

"Because," Wyatt said, "we'd still have to hike back up the mountain with our bikes, and then we'd have to make our way along the washed-out section of the trail. Or we'd have to head all the way back up to the overlook. Either way, by that time it will be dark. And I'm not even sure we can find our way back to the intermediate trail."

The animal path had seemed clear enough on the way down, but now that Wyatt looked back the way they had come, he had a hard time picking it out among the trees. And there had been a few spots where the path had branched and they had picked at random. How could they be sure they were even headed in the right direction?

"What are you trying to say, Wy?" Tanika asked.

Wyatt sighed. "I'm saying we're lost."

CHAPTER THREE

"How do people even get lost in a park?" Tanika grumbled. "It's not like we're in the uncharted wilderness. This park is, like, a thirty-minute drive from my home."

"At least we told our parents we were coming here," Wyatt said. "So if we don't make it home tonight, then they'll know where to send someone for us. Based on the warning sign, I'd guess we're at the very edge of the park, but that doesn't mean the park rangers are going to let us just get eaten by wild animals or starve to death."

Tanika raised an eyebrow. "Did you say 'if we don't make it home tonight'? We still probably have at least four hours before it gets dark. There is no way I'm spending the night in these woods."

"We might not have a choice," Wyatt said, though he didn't really like the thought either.

The sun wouldn't set for a while, but the clouds blocked most of the afternoon light. Wyatt was suddenly very aware of just how quiet the woods were. An occasional bird would call out in the distance, but other than that there was only the rustle of wind through the trees and the steady drip of water from the branches.

Tanika started talking as though she needed to fill the silence, and Wyatt was grateful. "Well, I don't know about you," she said, "but I didn't bring any camping gear with me. What's all in that backpack of yours? If you don't have a bike repair kit, then I suppose you don't have signal flares."

Wyatt tucked his damaged phone in a side pocket and looked through what was left. "I have the first aid kit, tire patch and pump, an extra granola bar, an extremely leaky water bottle, a small, not-so-sharp pocketknife that

I picked up at a garage sale, duct tape, and one of those cheap fold-up plastic ponchos."

Tanika nodded thoughtfully as he listed the contents. "Not bad. Is it one of those pocketknives with tools?"

"Yeah," Wyatt said. "But it's just stuff like a nail file, a screwdriver, a can opener, and a corkscrew. I can't really repair my bike with that."

"No," Tanika admitted, "but it helps to have options. And if we find any cans of food lying around, we'll be able to open them."

Wyatt gave a short chuckle.

"First things first—let's stop this water bottle from leaking anymore," Tanika said, reaching for the tire patch and sticking it over the hole. She nodded to herself in a satisfied way and looked back up at Wyatt.

"Well, what now?" he asked, trying to keep his voice more light and casual than he felt.

Tanika snorted. "That's all I've got! You're the big planner! Usually you'd have a color-coded checklist written up by now. So what's the plan for an emergency?"

"My *plan* for an emergency was to pack some extra things in my backpack and use my phone to call for help. I didn't exactly plan on something like this happening."

Tanika smiled grimly. "Who would?" She walked a couple of steps away and spun in a slow circle, surveying the surrounding woods for any sort of clue of which way they should go. "I guess it would make sense to head downhill, right?" she asked. "I know it's probably not technically part of the park property anymore, but we need to head back down the mountain anyway."

"Yeah," Wyatt agreed, "but the path goes up and down so much that we could think we were walking down, but actually be going in the opposite direction of the park entrance and the parking lot."

"Oh yeah, I see what you mean," Tanika said. She glanced up at the sky. "And of course it's so cloudy and foggy that we can't just use the sun as a point of reference."

"And we can't do the old sailor thing and navigate using the stars," Wyatt muttered.

Not that he knew what that involved, anyway.

"Is that trick you always see in movies accurate?" Tanika asked suddenly.

Wyatt felt like he had missed something. "What trick?"

"The thing where you see what side of the tree the moss is growing on," Tanika said, as though that should have been obvious.

Wyatt thought he remembered hearing something like that at one point, but he couldn't remember if it actually worked or if it was just an urban legend. "I don't know, but it's the best we've got to go on at the moment," he said.

"Okay," Tanika said, examining the trees nearby. "So let's say the moss is growing on the north side of the trees." She looked around and sighed. "A lot of these trees have moss on all sides, but it looks like it's thickest over here"—she gestured to the side of the tree facing Wyatt—"so that must be north."

"Makes sense to me," Wyatt said with a shrug. "And I'm pretty sure we want to go south and east from what I remember of where the sun was when we pulled into the parking lot."

Wyatt stood up, wincing, and walked over to his bike.

"What are you doing?" Tanika asked.

Wyatt stopped, puzzled. "I'm getting my bike."

"There's no way you're hauling that thing through the woods with your injured arm."

"I'm not leaving my bike," Wyatt said sharply. It was one of his most prized possessions, and there was no way he was just going to leave it in the woods to rust. It was badly damaged, but Wyatt was hoping the mechanic at the local bike shop could fix it. "You're taking *your* bike with you, I'm assuming?"

"Well, yeah, but my bike rolls," she said with a small laugh. She hung her helmet from the handlebars and flipped up the kickstand. "And if we reach one of the main trails, I can ride ahead for help."

"Yeah, well," Wyatt sputtered. As much as he hated to admit it, what Tanika said made a lot of sense. He huffed in exasperation. "Fine, as long as we can try to come back to find it later. You know, once we actually have a map and a working phone and more than a couple hours of daylight."

"I have an idea," Tanika said, smiling. She grabbed the duct tape out of Wyatt's backpack and used it to secure the orange warning sign to a small tree on the edge of the animal path. Then she laid Wyatt's bike carefully at the base of the tree. "See, this way the spot is marked, and the warning sign is back up where people can actually read it."

Wyatt smiled, thinking of how it would be easier to find his bike with a marker like the warning sign. "Looks good," he said.

"Maybe we could use that poncho to cover the bike to protect it from the elements?" Tanika offered.

"I'm tempted," Wyatt said, "but I'm thinking we better save the poncho for ourselves in case it starts pouring again like it did yesterday. I love that bike, but I care about our safety a lot more."

***

They trekked through the woods in the direction they hoped was southeast. Assuming that southeast even was the right direction. Wyatt knew they needed to remain calm. He tried telling himself that they were bound to find a road or a park ranger or something eventually, but he honestly wasn't convinced that was true.

The park didn't seem so big when they were speeding down the trails on their mountain bikes. But Wyatt had no idea how long it would take them to hike the same distance, especially with his injured arm and Tanika pushing her bike along. He guessed it was probably already well into the afternoon based on the amount of time they'd already been out on the trail. *We probably only have a few more hours until it starts to really get dark*, he thought to himself. And he wasn't eager to face the woods without the light of day. He remembered that the warning sign had mentioned dangerous terrain and unpredictable weather, but also—

"Did you know that we have *all* sorts of predators in the woods around here?" Tanika asked suddenly, as if she had been thinking the same thing.

"Isn't it just bears?" Wyatt asked.

"There are grizzly bears and black bears," Tanika said, ticking them off on her fingers, "but I'm pretty sure there are also wolves, coyotes, and mountain lions. Comforting thought, right?" she teased.

"Yeah," Wyatt said, his voice practically a whisper. "Thanks for the nature lesson." He glanced over his shoulder nervously, but there was nothing there.

Tanika suddenly spoke up in a loud, clear voice that made Wyatt jump. "I've always heard that the best way to avoid running into wild animals is to make a lot of noise," she said. "If you give them a heads up that you're coming, they're not going to be startled. And it's when they're startled that they get defensive and attack."

"Good thinking. And besides—" Wyatt started to say, then started again, louder this time, "*And besides*, if there's anyone else out in the woods, maybe they'll hear us."

He didn't add what he was thinking—that if they ended up stranded in the woods overnight and their parents called them in as missing, there would be search and rescue parties combing the woods. *And you want the search and rescue parties to be able to find you*, he thought. But he hoped it wouldn't come to that.

They walked on, talking about other things like upcoming pool parties and what teachers they would have next year. Anything to take their minds off their current situation.

But there was only so much Wyatt cared to talk about. And soon he started tuning out Tanika's chatter, thinking instead about the darkening clouds and the sounds of twigs snapping in the undergrowth.

CHAPTER FOUR

After about an hour, Wyatt stopped suddenly. "Hold up."

"What?" Tanika asked.

"I'm pretty sure we're going in circles," Wyatt said.

Tanika looked around. "Everything looks the same in these woods. How can you be sure?" she asked.

Wyatt pointed to a shallow cut in the bark of a nearby tree. "I've been using my pocketknife to mark trees every once in a while."

"Like a trail of bread crumbs," Tanika said.

"Exactly," Wyatt said grimly. "And we've passed by this tree before."

"How did we get turned around?" Tanika asked, annoyance ringing in her words. "I swear we were heading in a straight line."

"There were a couple times that we had to go around fallen trees, and we kept going left. Our turns must have added up until we ended up right back where we started."

"But how can we stop it from happening?" Tanika asked. Clearly his theory wasn't doing much to comfort her.

"What if we alternate between turning right and left around obstacles? That should help balance us out." Wyatt said.

Wyatt laid out a strategy about how to keep track of their direction and how to check at points along the way, but Tanika didn't seem at all interested in the details of his plan—or his lengthy explanation.

Once he finished talking, Tanika raised a bored eyebrow. "Did it really require that much explanation?"

"Uh." Wyatt didn't know what to say.

"You really need to learn how to get to the point, Wy," Tanika muttered.

She folded her arms across her chest, and Wyatt couldn't tell if it was out of annoyance or because she was cold. Probably a little bit of both. He knew she was probably just snapping at him because she was starting to get freaked out about the situation, but Wyatt thought it was a bit bold of her to be annoyed. Especially since Wyatt was the only one coming up with any real plans to get them out of the mess.

It's not my fault you have the attention span of a goldfish, he thought meanly.

They set out again, this time trying to be more aware of their surroundings and keeping an eye out for the marked trees as Wyatt had suggested. Wyatt was shivering a little bit.

Wyatt noticed that it was getting progressively darker as the sun sank lower in the sky and the clouds thickened. The weather had seemed great when they were on their bikes, but now it wasn't so nice, especially when the wind whipped through the trees and sent drops of cold water splattering down on the backs of their necks. Wyatt was tired and cold.

And all of a sudden it struck him that he was also incredibly thirsty.

His mouth was dry and he wondered how he could be this thirsty when the forest around them was so damp and foggy. He kicked the ground in frustration—his shoes were caked with mud.

Wyatt swung his backpack around and reached in for his water bottle. The inside of his bag was still sopping wet, and when he pulled out the bottle her understood why. The tire patch hadn't worked to fill the hole, and the rest of his water had slowly drained out of the bottle. Wyatt glared at the water bottle, as though that would somehow bring the water back. He felt his stomach clench as he thought about how much longer they would be able to last without water.

All the while, Tanika didn't notice a thing and kept up her nonstop chattering. Wyatt was more of the type to enjoy being *around* friends, but he didn't really feel a need to talk *to* them constantly. Usually he was grateful that Tanika could pick up the slack in their conversations, but at the moment the constant buzz was starting to get on his nerves.

"So," he interjected when she paused for breath. "What should we do about water?"

"Right?!" Tanika exclaimed. "I have been *so* thirsty for the past hour, but I didn't really want to bring it up because obviously you're in the same boat, and complaining about it didn't seem like it would help much." She indicated her empty water bottle hooked to her bike and frowned. "I mean, we already used my portion. But you still have some left." Then she spotted Wyatt holding up his empty water bottle. "Wait, what happened."

"Your patch didn't actually stop the water bottle from leaking. I'm completely empty as well." Wyatt tried and failed to keep the accusation out of his tone.

Tanika looked at him cautiously for a moment but didn't take the bait. "If we can find a way to get water, we can fill up my water bottle and share," Tanika offered.

"But how do we find water?" Wyatt asked, exasperated.

"I guess we look for some sort of body of water, like a pond or a creek," Tanika said, scanning the woods around her. "And just hope we stumble across one?"

Another drop of cold water hit Wyatt's neck and slithered down his back. He realized that it wasn't just the water blowing from the trees—it was actually sprinkling. *Great*, he thought. *Just what we need*. But then an idea came to him. "I guess we could try to tie up my poncho between the trees and use it to catch rainwater," he suggested.

Tanika held out her hand. "It's hardly even drizzling. It would take us ages to collect enough water that way. Being thirsty is terrible, but I don't know if we're *that* desperate yet. Wouldn't it be better to keep moving and try to find a way out of here? The longer we wait around, the more likely it is that we won't make it back before it gets dark."

Wyatt tried to swallow, but his throat felt too dry. He had to agree with Tanika. "Okay, then we keep moving, but we try to find a source of drinkable water."

Tanika gasped. "I just realized," she said, her words coming out in an excited jumble, "there was that creek. Back near the park entrance, like a five minute bike ride along the main road from the visitor center."

"Yeah, I remember it," Wyatt said. "We had to go single file to pass by those hikers that had stopped to take pictures on the bridge going over the creek. But how does that help us out here?"

Tanika continued, "If the creek has its source further up the mountain, and then flows south to eventually ends up near the visitor center . . ."

Suddenly, Wyatt understood. "Then we would just need to follow the creek and it will lead us back to the bridge," Wyatt finished. "That is genius, Tanika! But which direction do we go? I have no idea where the creek is in relation to where we are now."

Tanika bit her lip. "I know you're not going to want to hear this, Wy, but I think we need to turn your phone on. If we can consult the trail map—"

"But if my phone is still wet then there's a good chance that it will be busted entirely," Wyatt interrupted her. He knew it was unreasonable, but he felt his face flush with anger. How was it fair that Tanika could forget her phone in the car and then expect him to ruin his own phone?

"But if your phone works then we have a chance to look at the trail map and maybe find our way out of here," Tanika snapped.

"And if it doesn't work, we're back to square one," he shot back.

Tanika scowled. "Do you mean if your phone doesn't work because it's broken, or if your phone doesn't work because you're too stubborn to try turning it on?! We need to try *something*, Wy!"

Wyatt fumed but couldn't think of anything to say. Deep down he knew she was right.

He would feel like an idiot if they had to spend the night in the woods only to discover that his phone had been working the whole time. He dug it out of his backpack pocket.

There was no way to tell just from looking at it whether it had dried out enough to turn on. He held his breath as he as he held down the power button and let it out as a sigh of relief when the screen lit up.

"Thank goodness," he muttered.

"Should we call for help first?" Tanika asked.

Wyatt shook his head slowly. "I have absolutely no service out here. And I don't have data access either, so I can't message anyone." He opened the screenshot of the trail map.

The map wasn't detailed enough to figure out exactly where they were just by looking, but if they could figure out where they had left the intermediate trail, maybe they could work their way backward.

"Okay, here is the trail," Wyatt said, tracing the blue line with his finger. We must have left the path before we reached the black diamond trail, because we never saw a sign for it." He pointed to the yellow line that branched off from the blue one. "We had biked pretty far from the overlook up here," he said, pointing to the symbol on the map closer to the top of the mountain. "So we were somewhere in between those two landmarks."

Tanika peered over his shoulder. "Look!" she said, stopping just short of jabbing the screen with her finger in excitement. "This spot here, where the trail twists left, goes back to the right, and then there's a chain of three jumps. I definitely remember that part, and it was right before we ran into the part of the trail that was washed out. So we must have left the trail somewhere around here." She pointed to a bend in the blue line.

Wyatt grimaced when he saw how close they had been to the actual advanced trail. If they had just walked their bikes a little farther . . . but it didn't do them any good now to think about that.

"And there's the creek," Wyatt said. "You were right, it starts higher up in the mountain, then snakes down and around before crossing the bridge here, near the visitor center. So assuming we're somewhere in here"—he indicated the large gray "off limits" area—"we just need to head south until we hit the creek, then follow it east until we reach the bridge. From there we can join up with the main road until we hit the visitor center."

Tanika froze suddenly. "Wy, look, you have a bar," she whispered, as though she were afraid the cell service would bolt like a frightened animal if she spooked it.

Wyatt's heart skipped a beat. If he could make a call, they might be able to get out of this mess without even having to find the creek. The number for the park ranger was listed at the bottom of the trail map.

Hands shaking, trying not to move the phone too much in case it could only pick up the signal in this one square inch of space, he dialed the number.

Just as he pressed "call," the low battery warning flashed, and the phone started to shut down.

"No, no, no, no!" he muttered. How had he not noticed that the battery level was critical when he turned it on? He desperately tapped the screen, but the phone powered off anyway.

He pressed the power button again, but there was no sign of life. "No, no, no, oh please, c'mon, please work." But he knew it was no use. He tried to resist the urge to chuck his phone against the nearest tree trunk.

Tanika's eyes were wide. "Look, Wy—" she started quietly.

"I don't want to hear it, Tanika, okay?" Wyatt snapped. "We have a better idea of where the creek is, sure. That's great. Doesn't change the fact that now we have absolutely no working phones. If we had waited, maybe we could have gotten to some place with better signal and actually called for help."

"I didn't think—" Tanika started.

"Yeah, well maybe you should have done some more thinking before you forgot your phone in the car," Wyatt said. "*Again.*"

Tanika's mouth pressed into a flat line. Her eyes flashed, but there was hurt mixed with the anger.

Part of Wyatt wished he could take back what he said, but another overwhelming part of him was too tired and thirsty to care.

"We go south to the get to the creek, right?" Tanika said through clenched teeth.

"Yeah," Wyatt muttered. "Then we follow it east."

"Let's get going then," she said. "Before we die of thirst, preferably," she added bitterly.

"We should stay quiet so we can listen for sounds of running water," Wyatt said, unable to bring himself to meet her eye. "We might be able to hear the creek from a distance."

"Good," Tanika fumed as she grabbed her bike and started walking. "I wasn't planning on talking to you anyway."

CHAPTER FIVE

The next hour passed in agonizing silence, broken only by their heavy breathing as they climbed up ridges and picked their way carefully down slopes, occasionally slipping on an especially slick layer of dead pine needles in the evening glow of the setting sun.

Wyatt tried to ignore the fact that his arm was still bleeding and a dark red blotch had soaked through the bandage. Between that and how thirsty he still was, Wyatt was thankful that Tanika didn't seem willing to break her silence. As much as he hated to admit it, Wyatt was pretty sure he was the one who had overreacted. But he wasn't in the mood to apologize for being a jerk. So silence was easier.

When Wyatt finally heard a low burble almost beyond the edge of hearing, he hardly dared to believe it. Maybe it was just his pulse pumping in his own ears. Finding the creek drastically increased their chances of making it out of the woods, Wyatt knew. And after the series of bad luck that afternoon, he found it hard to believe that they had found the creek in under an hour.

But Tanika seemed to have heard it too because she stopped suddenly, her eyes lit up as she turned to Wyatt, her anger with him temporarily forgotten.

In a split second the excitement in her eyes changed to horror, and she stared over Wyatt's shoulder at something behind him. Her mouth dropped open, and she looked like she wanted to scream but was too afraid to let it out.

Wyatt felt his blood run cold as he slowly turned his head to see what it was that had scared Tanika. And he didn't like what he saw.

A mountain lion was crouched on a rock about thirty feet away.

As Wyatt's breath caught in his throat, his mind raced wildly. They had passed *right* by it without seeing it. How had they not noticed? It definitely had noticed *them*.

The mountain lion stared intently at them, but Wyatt couldn't tell if it was sizing them up as prey, or if it was just curious what they were doing in its habitat.

Wyatt felt frozen, and he heard Tanika's voice as if from a long way off.

"Wy," she was saying, her voice a low, urgent hiss. "*Wyatt*, what do we do? I can't remember what you're supposed to do if you see a mountain lion."

Wyatt thought he'd heard something about mountain lions somewhere, but fear had turned his mind to sludge and he couldn't seem to think of the advice, let alone get any words out.

They had both turned slowly to face the mountain lion, and that sparked a memory for Wyatt. "Whatever you do, don't turn your back on it and don't run," he croaked, "or its instinct will be to chase us."

"What else are we supposed to do?" Tanika prompted.

"I, I don't know," Wyatt said. Why couldn't he think? His frustration at being frozen with fear only made it harder to move, and his heart seemed to thump wildly against his bruised chest.

The mountain lion crouched lower, its tail twitching slowly, almost lazily. It put a tentative paw forward, easing toward them smoothly. One step, then another—never taking its eyes off them.

"What's it doing? What does that mean? Wyatt, is it going to attack us?" Tanika asked so rapidly that her words smooshed together.

Wyatt scrunched his eyes shut, trying to remember what they were supposed to do. And then it clicked. His eyes sprung open. "We need to look big and scary. That way it will know we're human and not prey. Humans aren't worth their time. Mountain lions don't usually attack humans."

"Usually?" Tanika squeaked.

The mountain lion had moved again, closing the distance between them. Fifteen feet away, it stopped and continued to stare at them. Wyatt was all too aware of the powerful muscles that rippled under the mountain lion's fur whenever it moved. That thing could pounce and take them down easily if it decided they were prey.

"How are we supposed to be bigger and scarier than that thing?" Tanika asked.

Wyatt's throat was tight with fear, but Tanika's focus was keeping him from completely losing it. "Uh, we've got to—you're supposed to—we need to make a lot of noise, raise our arms over our head, and try to be loud enough to scare it off."

Wyatt found that was easier said than done. In that moment, his panicked brain wouldn't let him do it. Every instinct was telling him to run and hide or to freeze and hope the predator didn't see him. Running from it would be a death wish, but shouting at the mountain lion seemed just as foolish.

Tanika's voice cut through the foggy woods as she began to sing. It was just something they had heard on the radio as they were parking that morning, but she belted it out. She quickly unclipped her bike helmet from the handlebars and tapped it against her bike to make a loud clanging noise.

"Wyatt, make some sort of noise," Tanika said, then continued to sing loudly.

Wyatt couldn't remember the lyrics to the song Tanika was singing, but her bravery calmed him down enough that he managed to join in with a song that he did know. And although he couldn't match Tanika's volume and confidence, the combination of the two songs made a loud jumble of noise that the mountain lion didn't seem to enjoy. It started to back away from them. But it didn't look scared, just mildly annoyed.

Wyatt felt a little ridiculous singing at a mountain lion in the middle of the woods, but it boosted his courage.

At last the mountain lion seemed to give up, and it slunk back into the bushes. It turned to look at them once more, but Tanika sang louder and the mountain lion continued to head back the way it came. It moved leisurely, as if it had decided they were too boring to waste time on.

Wyatt wanted to sigh with relief, but he hardly dared to breathe. He still wasn't entirely convinced that the mountain lion wouldn't come back.

"That was so intense," Tanika said, grinning widely.

"Why are you smiling?" Wyatt asked in disbelief, keeping his eyes on the place they had last seen the mountain lion. "That thing could have killed us!"

"I know," Tanika said, "but we scared it off! That was such a rush. Better than landing a really good jump on your bike."

Wyatt wanted to point out that the mountain lion hadn't been scared of them, but he was glad that she seemed to have forgotten how much of a jerk he was earlier, and he didn't want to start another argument with her.

She scanned the woods around them. "So . . . how long do we have to wait before we can keep going?"

Wyatt was still trying to relax each muscle that had tightened up in fear moments before. He couldn't understand how Tanika didn't even seem phased. He rolled his head around to loosen his neck a few times before responding. "Uhh, I think since the mountain lion headed off in the other direction, we're safe to keep walking. We just need to make enough noise this time. And watch our backs."

"I think we're almost to the creek, at least," Tanika said. She pointed suddenly at the trees, grinning again. "Look! I think I can see it!"

Wyatt squinted the way she was pointing and could just make out rushing water in between the trees. And for the first time in the last few hours, Wyatt felt like grinning himself. They finally knew where they were again.

CHAPTER SIX

The creek flowed swiftly between its banks. Wyatt licked his chapped lips at the sight of so much water.

Tanika unhooked her water bottle from the side of her bike and unscrewed the top.

"Wait," Wyatt said, "we can't just drink that water."

Tanika stared him down. "I'm thirstier than I've ever been, and we escaped a mountain lion to find this creek in the first place."

"But we could get sick if we don't disinfect the water," Wyatt insisted. Although, the longer he thought about his own thirst the less of an argument he felt he had.

"It's moving water," Tanika reasoned. "Sure, if this was some gross, muddy pond, we'd have something to worry about, but look at how crystal clear the water is!"

"It's still going to have bacteria in it," Wyatt protested.

"And besides," Tanika continued, "there is no way that we have time to stop and disinfect it. We're running out of daylight as it is."

"Yeah," Wyatt said reluctantly. "I guess you're right. Disinfecting it would involve us building a fire—"

"Which we would have no way to light," Tanika interjected.

"—and boiling the water for ten minutes—"

"Which would mean finding a container to boil the water in." Tanika rolled her eyes. "C'mon, Wy, we need to get our priorities straight."

Wyatt gave a defeated sigh. "Okay, go ahead, but only take small sips. And don't blame me if you get stomach cramps later."

Tanika was already dipping the water bottle in the cool mountain creek before Wyatt had finished his warning. They passed the water bottle back and forth, drinking as much as they dared, then they filled the bottle again and packed it up.

The mountain creek was so cold that the water gave him a brain freeze, but Wyatt didn't think water had ever tasted so good. And Tanika was right—they didn't have the time to play it safe or do everything by the book like he would have preferred.

"So now we just follow the creek out of here, right?" Tanika asked.

"Yeah, I think so," Wyatt said. "And if we were right about the creek being south of where I crashed, then we know for sure that we're facing south right now. Which means we have to go east along the creek to get to the bridge."

"That doesn't sound so bad," Tanika said. "As long as we don't run into any more mountain lions." She held up her crossed fingers.

Wyatt wished he had her optimism, but he was still shaken from seeing the mountain lion, and the cut on his arm was still stinging painfully with every move. But he forced a smile for the benefit of his friend. "No problem at all."

***

Wyatt had assumed that once they found the creek, it would be an easy walk back to the visitor center.

And while it was comforting to have the sound of the rushing water as a reminder that they were on the right path, he found the walk tiring and long.

The distances on the map must not have been to scale. *Or maybe*, Wyatt thought with growing concern, *we got the directions mixed up and are following the creek further into the wild.* He tried to remember what the trail map had looked like. But there hadn't been much detail put into the off limits part of the map since visitors weren't expected to be out there in the first place. All Wyatt knew was that they really needed to be heading the right direction. The sun was sinking faster and faster in the sky.

In the growing dusk, Tanika narrowly avoided tripping over an exposed root and slipping down into the creek. Shapes had become hard to distinguish and the colors started to fade until everything looked gray in the gloom.

Tanika caught herself and turned on her bike's headlight. In this strange twilight, it hardly did any good, but they would be thankful for it as soon as night fell. Which, Wyatt guessed with a sinking feeling, would probably be in the next half hour, maybe sooner. And they still had no way of knowing how close they were to the bridge, or even if they were going in the right direction.

Tanika stopped abruptly, the comfortingly familiar rustle of her bike tires over the dead pine needles falling silent, immediately putting Wyatt on edge.

"What is it?" Wyatt asked, scanning the woods around them nervously, half expecting to see another mountain lion.

"This isn't working," Tanika said.

"What isn't?" Wyatt asked.

"*This,*" Tanika said, gesturing at the creek. "How can we even be sure we're going the right way? Shouldn't we have run into that bridge by now?"

Wyatt was glad he hadn't been the only one to have that thought.

"It could still be the right way," he argued, mostly because he was too terrified to admit that they might have spent valuable hours of daylight heading the wrong direction. "Maybe the bridge is just farther away than we thought."

Tanika gazed up at the treetops. "I can't see anything down here in the middle of all these trees. How about I climb one of them and see if I can get a good look ahead? I might even be able to see the bridge from here. Or at least some sort of landmark, like lights from one of the nearby towns, so we at least know if we're heading toward civilization."

"That sounds like a horrible idea!" Wyatt blurted out, mostly because the thought of climbing a tree that high made his legs feel like jelly.

Tanika rolled her eyes in exasperation. "Do you have a better idea? I'm a great climber, and these pine trees have a lot of nice, straight branches."

"The branches are sturdy enough down at this level," Wyatt admitted, "but once you get up higher, who knows. I'm not even sure you'll be able to see anything from up there besides more trees."

"It's worth a shot," Tanika said, shrugging.

"No, it's *not* worth it," Wyatt countered. "What happens if you fall? If you get seriously injured, we have no way to get you help. How would I get us out of here?"

"You worry too much," Tanika said, heading toward the tree.

"Tanika, wait!" Wyatt groaned. "Stop, seriously, what are you even doing? *Tanika!*"

Wyatt bit his lip. Tanika's lack of fear had been getting her into trouble as long as Wyatt had known her. And in a survival situation like this, it could get her hurt . . . or worse.

Tanika pulled herself up into the lowest branches and started to climb. Wyatt called down for her to stop a few more times, but she was either ignoring him or too focused on the climb to pay attention to his warnings.

It looked like Tanika had been right that the branches made for good climbing. Within a minute she was up higher than Wyatt would have dared to climb.

But as he stepped back to keep his eye on her, Wyatt thought that maybe Tanika's plan had a chance of working. This particular tree stood a little apart from the others on the creek bank, and it was taller. Wyatt sighed. He would never hear the end of it if Tanika's daredevil plan worked, but he didn't really want her to fail either because of what *that* would mean.

"Can you see anything?" he called after a while. He could only just see Tanika's bright jacket up among the branches of the tree.

Wyatt heard nothing for a moment, then Tanika gave an excited shout.

"I do, Wy! I can't see the bridge from here because it's hidden by the trees, but I can totally see the visitor center building and bit of the parking lot. It's still a little ways off, but we're heading in the right direction!"

Wyatt breathed a sigh of relief that safety might literally be in sight. If they got out of this without having to spend the night in the woods, he would be *so* grateful.

"It's really beautiful up here," Tanika shouted. "You can see the last bit of sunset and the first stars and the—"

"Great," Wyatt shouted sarcastically, "but stars mean nightfall, which means trying to find our way in pitch blackness. We can stargaze once we get out of these woods! Now get down before you hurt yourself."

Wyatt swore he could feel Tanika's eyes rolling at him. Soon he heard the rustling sound of movement in the tree, and Tanika came back into view.

Tanika seemed pleased with herself as she climbed down.

"I told you so!" she called cheerfully. And a split second later, she was falling.

CHAPTER SEVEN

Wyatt saw it all happen as if it was in slow motion. Tanika's foot scraped the trunk for a foothold, but the sole of her sneaker slipped, sending a shower of bark raining down. Tanika shrieked and lost her balance. She slid down the tree, unable to grab anything to break her fall.

She had climbed down low enough that she didn't have very far to fall, but she still landed hard. Wyatt had seen enough mountain bike crashes—at least on social media—to recognize a bad fall when he saw it. His breath caught in his throat. Tanika had landed in a half crouch, but now she rolled over onto her side, grasping her leg.

"Tanika!" Wyatt yelled as he rushed toward her. He knew from the way she was gritting her teeth and had her eyes squeezed shut that it would be pointless to ask if she was okay. So instead he asked, "How bad is it? What did you hurt?"

"My ankle," Tanika managed to say without unclenching her teeth or opening her eyes.

Wyatt looked at Tanika's ankle. It was already swelling and bruising, but the ankle wasn't twisted at an odd angle, so that was good.

"Can you move it?" Wyatt asked.

Tanika grimaced. "I think I *could*, but that doesn't mean I *want* to." She groaned. "I'm not sure I can stand, though. It made kind of a popping sound, not a cracking sound, so I'm really hoping it's a sprain and not a fracture."

Now that he knew Tanika hadn't been seriously hurt in the fall, Wyatt couldn't resist teasing her. "Would you be mad if I said 'I told you so' right now?" he said, giving her a friendly smirk.

Tanika groaned, but this time in mock annoyance. "Just help me up, Wy," she grumbled.

Wyatt let her put her arm around his shoulders, then carefully stood up, supporting her as she balanced on one wobbly leg, holding her swollen ankle away from the ground.

Tanika shifted her weight, then bit back a yelp of pain. "In case you were wondering," she said with a straight face, "the answer is no—I can't put weight on that leg."

Wyatt helped her hobble over to the tree trunk so she could balance on her own for a second. "There's no way you're going to be able to push your bike in this condition."

Tanika frowned. "But we already came this far with it. Maybe it will help me walk. Like a set of crutches with wheels."

"Maybe if we were just walking down the block, but there's no way you'll be able to do that in the woods. It's going to be hard enough to make it to the bridge as it is, without lugging the bike with us. It's like you said with my bike. We're just going to have to come back for it."

Tanika's eyebrows knitted together anxiously. "I guess . . ." she said reluctantly. "I just don't want to leave my baby here." She sighed. "I know, I know, we don't really have a choice. But we should grab the headlight and my water bottle. And anything else that might be useful."

"I wish we had some way to set your ankle," Wyatt mused. "If it's broken, then we want to keep it from moving. I guess I could use a part from your bike as a splint if we strapped it to your leg with the bandages from the first aid kit."

Wyatt swore he could see Tanika's eyes flash even in the dim light.

"Don't you dare, Wy!" she said. "I already agreed to leave my bike here, but there is no way you are stripping her for parts! Especially not with that dinky little multi-tool on your pocketknife."

Wyatt chuckled. "Don't worry, I won't. I'm not sure it would even do any good. And besides, we're finally within reach of the bridge. It will be slow going, but at least we know we're close and going in the right direction."

"And we have the bike headlight," Tanika added, her voice shaking as she stared at the dark woods around them.

For the first time all day, Tanika didn't sound sure of herself. Wyatt realized that her positive outlook had been helping him stay calm. Now that her confidence was shaken, his stomach felt tight with anxiety. *I'll just have to be brave for both of us*, he thought.

"Hey," he said kindly, "we'll be fine. Just take it slow, lean on me, and do your best to keep the headlight pointed at the ground in front of us. The last thing I want is for us to trip. We're banged up enough as it is," he said.

If anything, the forest was louder at night than it had been during the day. Wyatt had thought the sounds would be comforting after the damp stillness of the afternoon, but he found himself jumping at every small sound.

He had no idea what sorts of creatures made the sounds he was hearing, and he wasn't sure he wanted to find out. The rational part of his brain told him that they were probably all frogs or insects or owls, but some of them sounded otherworldly. Chatting hadn't seemed too out of place in the daylight, but now that the dark pressed in around them, Wyatt found it hard to speak above a loud whisper.

The whitish circle of light from the headlight didn't do much to relieve his fears. It lit the path in front of them and kept them from tripping over roots and rocks, but outside of its glow the forest seemed even darker by comparison. From time to time, Wyatt thought he saw shadows move in the dark or the greenish glow of the light hitting some creature's eyes, but it might have just been his imagination. After all, he was beyond exhausted. All he wanted was to tumble into his bed and pull up the warm covers. Instead, he was dealing with the blisters forming on his feet and nothing but his thin blue jacket to keep him warm.

It was hard to tell distance in the dark, and Wyatt had never noticed how much he depended on his phone as a clock. He was

losing track of time, and for all he knew
they had been struggling along in the dark
for hours. He was glad the creek made noise
because he could barely see it anymore. But as
long as they kept that sound to their right, they
would have to reach the bridge sooner or later.
And Wyatt hoped it would be sooner.

Their progress was slow, with Tanika using
Wyatt as a makeshift crutch and whimpering
in pain whenever she accidentally put pressure
on her ankle or brushed against a rock or root
with her dangling foot.

"Ugh, it's probably broken," she muttered.
"That would be just my luck."

"Just try not to think about it. Keep your
mind on other things . . . like the dark and the
wild animals," Wyatt teased

Tanika snorted. "You should put that
on an inspirational poster—'Just think about
all the other things that could make your
situation *worse!*'"

Wyatt gave a small chuckle.

A branch cracked loudly somewhere in
the forest off to their left. Wyatt and Tanika

both froze for a moment, listening intently and hardly daring to breathe. Wyatt's heart pounded against his rib cage, and he felt himself trembling—like he was a little kid scared of the dark.

"It's probably just a deer or something, right?" he whispered to Tanika after a long moment.

"Yeah," she said, taking in a shaky breath. "It's probably *not* a dangerous predator coming to finish us off." She gave him a small, tight-lipped smile.

"Well, we aren't worth the trouble," Wyatt pointed out. "There is plenty of other tastier prey out there."

He tried to take some comfort from his reasoning. Logic seemed like a good counter to the fear he was feeling. But that didn't stop hairs on the back of his neck from prickling uneasily as they resumed their slow hobble toward the bridge.

CHAPTER EIGHT

Wyatt could hardly believe that over the course of the day, he had gone from jumping obstacles on his mountain bike to staggering through the wilderness, bloodied, bruised, and terrified.

He was just glad that he and Tanika had stuck together in spite of their arguments. He wasn't sure he would have been able to face this without her. If he had been alone, he would have had a hard time convincing himself not to whip together a makeshift tent out of his poncho, curl up in the fetal position, and lie awake shivering until morning.

In the dark, they almost didn't see the bridge until they were right at it. Wyatt helped

Tanika up the short incline from the creek bank to the wooden bridge. After their time in the woods, it was a relief to have a manmade structure under their feet again.

Wyatt helped Tanika sit down to rest for a little bit before they made it the rest of the way. He looked at her, and they shared a shaky, tired laugh, hardly daring to believe that they had finally made it back to the path.

"I can't wait until we get back to the car," Tanika said.

"Or until I get home and take a shower," Wyatt said. He couldn't imagine how ragged they must look right now, with torn, bloody clothes and makeshift bandages. He shifted his arm and winced as pain shot up along his elbow. "I'm just glad we're—"

He heard the growl before he saw the mountain lion. Wyatt jumped up. They were halfway across the bridge, and it was standing at the end closest to the woods. The way to the Visitor Center was open, but Wyatt knew that if they tried to make a run for it they wouldn't stand a chance, and besides, Tanika wouldn't be able to make it more than a few steps before her ankle would most likely give out beneath her.

"Do you think that's the same mountain lion from before?" Wyatt asked.

"I don't know!" Tanika snapped. "Do you want me to see if it has a collar and a name tag?" She pulled herself up using Wyatt's arm and braced herself against the bridge railing. "Hey! You!" she shouted at the mountain lion. "Get out of here! Bad kitty!"

Wyatt unclipped his helmet and whacked it against the railing on the other side of the bridge. But if this was the same mountain lion from before, it now seemed completely unconcerned by the noise they were making. Wyatt looked around desperately for anything to fight off the mountain lion with as it prowled closer to them, its eyes flashing green in the light from their headlight.

It was only twenty feet away from them. Wyatt wondered how far mountain lions could pounce in a single leap.

Fifteen feet away. They had nothing to fight it with. They couldn't even use Tanika's bike as a shield since they had left it behind. And Tanika herself was in no shape to do much more than yell. She was shouting as loudly as she could, but Wyatt could see her wincing in pain.

Usually Wyatt would look to Tanika to be the one to come up with some wild impulsive idea that would save them. But Wyatt knew now that if he didn't come up with a strategy, they might not make it back to the parking lot.

Wyatt's brain buzzed. His muscles were so wound up he felt like he could barely move. He forced himself to take deep breaths, even though he felt like hyperventilating.

The mountain lion twitched its tail, a growl building low in its throat, a deep bass rumble that was almost too low to hear.

"What do we do, Wy?" Tanika asked. "I don't think it's working this time."

"I think we'll have to fight it off," Wyatt answered.

"*What?*" Tanika shot back. "With what, exactly?"

"I mean I guess we could break off a stick or something—"

"Hit it with your helmet," Tanika interrupted. "That thing is pretty hard. If you swing your helmet and smack it in the face, maybe it will decide we're not worth the trouble."

It was about as good an idea as any. The mountain lion opened its mouth and snarled at them, showing sharp teeth that gleamed in the glow from their headlight.

Wyatt stopped banging his helmet on the railing and let it dangle from his uninjured hand.

He watched the mountain lion's every move closely, ready to jump into action at the first sign of trouble. Wyatt's eyes darted between the swishing tail, the small turn of an ear, the legs that were bunched up like a coiled spring, ready to explode forward in a flurry of teeth and claws at any second. Meanwhile, he kept forcing himself to take slow, deep breaths. In and out. In and out. Each breath an effort of willpower.

The mountain lion lunged, and Wyatt's reflexes were almost too slow to counter. He swung the helmet with all the strength he could muster. For a split second he thought that his wild swing had missed and that he would find himself pinned down under the mountain lion, its teeth ripping into him. But then the helmet connected with the mountain lion's face with a loud *thwack*, and the big cat jerked backward, hissing angrily.

"Yeah, that's right!" Wyatt shouted, startling both the cat and himself with his sudden confidence. "You leave me and my friend alone, got that?"

The cat took a step back, startled by the swinging helmet. But it was still snarling. Wyatt knew that it was only a matter of time before it tried to pounce again, and he wasn't sure how long his helmet would last against a 120-pound cat.

Just then, over the growl of the mountain lion, Wyatt heard something else. The hum of a motor and the crunch of tires on gravel.

Car headlights swung into view around the bend in the road, almost blinding after the darkness of the woods. Wyatt and Tanika squinted in the sudden burst of light. The mountain lion's tail twitched uneasily at the intrusion.

The car horn began to sound, the piercing beeps punctuated by flashing brights from the headlight. The mountain lion had clearly had enough. It turned, its claws scrabbling on the wood planks of the bridge, and bounded away into the woods.

The horn fell silent. A car door slammed, and a park ranger got out of the jeep, which was marked Evergreen Wilds Park Security. "Wyatt and Tanika?" she asked as she stepped around to the front of the car. "You kids all right?"

CHAPTER NINE

"You have no idea how perfect your timing is!" Tanika exclaimed with a relieved look on her face.

"How did you know to come look for us?" Wyatt asked.

"Your parents called the park when you weren't home by sundown."

Wyatt felt a twinge of guilt that they had scared their parents, but he was thankful that they had known to call the park. If the ranger hadn't shown up, he wasn't sure how they would have dealt with the mountain lion. But Wyatt suspected they wouldn't have made it out so easily.

The park ranger's walkie-talkie squawked, and she replied. "Yeah, it's fine, I found them. They're hurt but not in critical condition as far as I can tell."

There was another burst of static from the radio.

"I'll drive them back. Can you get the first aid station prepped? I'll need to get a better look, but I think we'll be able to patch them up with the supplies we have on site."

Wyatt helped Tanika into the jeep, letting her stretch her injured leg out on the back seat. Then he climbed into the front and the park ranger drove them back to the Evergreen Wilds Visitor Center. The warm glow of the electric lights was a welcome sight after the dark of the woods.

The on-site nurse handed them drinks and packets of trail mix, which they accepted gratefully. Then he reapplied the bandage on Wyatt's arm and checked his head for signs of a concussion.

The park ranger asked them questions about everything that had happened that afternoon while the nurse examined Tanika's bruised and swollen ankle.

Tanika launched into the story of their ordeal, complete with blow-by-blow descriptions of how they had fought off a mountain lion—twice.

The park ranger's expression alternated between concern and wide-eyed amazement.

"Well, you're safe now," she said, "thank goodness."

"I already called your parents to let them know you're all right," the nurse added. "They should be here to pick you up soon."

"I'm sorry," Wyatt blurted out, turning to Tanika.

Tanika raised her eyebrows. "For what?" she asked.

"For being a jerk," Wyatt explained. Wasn't that obvious? "You're one of my best friends. And it seems really stupid to ruin all that just because you forget your phone sometimes." He gave Tanika a sheepish smile, which she returned.

"I'm sorry too," Tanika said, wrinkling her

nose. "I definitely contributed to the stupid arguments. I'm still going to forget my phone sometimes. But I'll always make sure I have enough water with me," she smirked.

Wyatt snorted. "And maybe next time I should bring a paper trail map." He realized that the park ranger and nurse were listening to this whole conversation with amusement.

"It was kind of a long day," Wyatt explained to them.

"I'll bet," the park ranger said kindly. "We'll get that warning sign repaired and add a few more. And we'll see about relocating that mountain lion to a safer place away from humans. In the meantime, I think we should be able to figure out where you had to abandon your bikes and return them to you soon."

Wyatt felt relief wash over him. It would take the bike shop a while to repair all the damage on his bike, but it was still better than having to save up to buy a new one. Tanika grinned excitedly.

***

A couple of minutes later, Wyatt and Tanika sat at one of the tables in the Evergreen Wilds Visitor Center café. The park ranger made it clear she didn't think they were in any state to drive themselves. And Wyatt had to agree. So they sat together under shiny silver emergency blankets eating trail mix while they waited for their parents to arrive. With all they had gone through that afternoon, Wyatt had hardly noticed how hungry he was. He ripped open a second packet of trail mix.

"It doesn't seems possible that all of that just happened," Tanika said, leaning back in her chair. Her injured leg was propped up on a second chair, an ice pack wrapped around her ankle.

"But somehow, we survived." Wyatt folded his non-injured arm on the table and rested his head. "Yay, us," he mumbled sleepily.

He was glad that the only thing he had left to worry about was repairing his bike. Normal, everyday stress seemed much more manageable now that he no longer had to worry about his survival.

About the Author

Raelyn Drake thinks the Midwest is pretty swell, even if it's noticeably lacking in mountains. When she and her husband aren't traveling, they live in Minneapolis, Minnesota, with their rescue corgi mix, Sheriff.

X TO THE LIMIT

OFF ROAD

ON EDGE

RIPTIDE

WHITEOUT

WHEN THERE'S NO CHOICE BUT
TO PUSH IT TO THE EXTREME

DAY OF
DISASTER

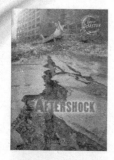

Would you survive?

ATTACK ON EARTH

**WHEN ALIENS INVADE,
ALL YOU CAN DO IS SURVIVE.**

DESERTED

THE FALLOUT

THE FIELD TRIP

GETTING HOME

LOCKDOWN

TAKE SHELTER

MASON FALLS MYSTERIES

EVEN AN ORDINARY TOWN HAS ITS SECRETS.